Moll

John B.
KEANE

Moll

MERCIER PRESS
IRISH PUBLISHER – IRISH STORY

MERCIER PRESS
Cork
www.mercierpress.ie

Original three act version first published 1969
This two act version first published 1988
This edition, 2011

© John B. Keane, 1991

ISBN: 978 1 78117 274 2
10 9 8 7 6 5 4 3 2 1

A CIP record for this title is available from the British Library

Moll is a copyright play and may not be performed without a licence.
Application for a licence for amateur performances must be made in
advance. Terms for professional performances may be had from JBK
Occasions, 37 William Street, Listowel, Co. Kerry.

Printed and bound in the EU.

CONTENTS

CHARACTERS   6

ACT ONE   7

    Bridge Act One, Scene One to Scene Two   20
    Bridge Act One, Scene Two to Scene Three   33
    Bridge Act One, Scene three to Scene Four   42

ACT TWO   46

    Bridge Act Two, Scene One to Scene Two   65

CHARACTERS

This revised version of *Moll* was first presented by Groundwork in association with Gaiety Entertainments at the Gaiety Theatre on 10 June 1991

Father Brest	Barry McGovern
Bridgie Andover	Joan Brosnan Walsh
Canon Pratt	Mick Lally
Father Loran	Ronan Smith
Moll	Pat Leavy
Ulick	Micheál Ó Briain
The Bishop	Derry Power

Director	Brian de Salvo
Designer	Bláithín Sheerin
Lighting	Rupert Murray
Producers	Ben Barnes
	Arthur Lappin
Executive producer	Ronan Smith

New revised text edited by Ben Barnes

ACT ONE

SCENE 1

To set a scene or provide an amusing philosophical commentary on the preceding one, a series of extracts from Canon Pratt's diary have been selected with appropriate accompanying action on the fore-stage. These 'front cloth' vignettes also enable the stage to be set for the following scene and ensure a continual flow of action.

Pratt   After the new money came things were never the same at the presbytery. Till then summers came and summers went each one much like the last. Ballast was a poor parish but God was good and even the weather was good sometimes and we went about our duties without a bother on us.

Until the summer of that fateful year of our Lord 1971 when the money went decimal. Oh it had a most shocking and deleterious effect on some people. Why else would our housekeeper of twenty years, the honest, sober, industrious and respectable Letitia Bottomley suddenly up and marry an American tourist and emigrate to New Jersey in the United States of America, there to open a diner which she entitled 'The Black Bottom Bistro'?

Yirra, 'twas the decimal money that drove the poor woman demented and left us with the onerous duty of finding a new housekeeper …

The curtain rises to reveal the dining cum sitting-room

of the parochial house in the town and parish of Ballast. Seated at one end of a large table to left of audience but facing them for the most part are three priests. Two are young whereas the one in the middle is elderly and exhibits the purple of a canon here and there. Seated at the other end of the table at right of audience but fully facing them is a large, dour woman of advanced years. She is Miss Andover. She wears hat and coat and has a large handbag held tightly in front of her. The curates are Fr Loran, the younger and Fr Brest, the older. The parish priest is Canon Pratt. In front of the priests are neat files to which they resort from time to time. As the curtain rises the priests and canon are seen to be exchanging whispers and confidences. Miss Andover strains forward trying to catch what they are saying. Fr Brest becomes aware of this and alerts the others who immediately pay full attention to Miss Andover.
Time: One morning not too long ago.

Fr Brest   It says here, Miss Andover, in this most recent reference from the late Fr Hennessy that you take a drink on occasion. Does this mean intoxicating drink?

Miss Andover   *(Looks away when she answers)* For all I take of it father, I don't know why he mentioned it at all, the Lord be good to the man.

Fr Brest   Yes, yes … You do take intoxicating drink however?

Miss Andover   On very rare occasions father, barring I had a cold or pains or the like.

Fr Brest   I see. *(To others)* Any further questions?

Canon Pratt   Supposing you were to get the job Miss Andover, would you require extra help?

Miss Andover   Well, I would have to have a maid naturally. There's

8

	three of you ….
Canon Pratt	And what sort of salary would you be expecting?
Miss Andover	God knows canon seeing the way everything's gone up since the money went decimal if I get's the job, I'd need ten pounds a week.
Fr Brest	It says here, Miss Andover, that you are a good, natural cook.
Miss Andover	I'm all that father.
Fr Brest	I'm sure you are. Tell me. What is meant by *natural?*
Miss Andover	Yirra, the Lord be good to the poor man father, he always ate what I put in front of him and there was never a word out of him.
Fr Brest	I'm sure he did. It's just that the expression is so unusual. *(To others)* These are not the kind of words that automatically link each other. Usually we hear of plain cooks and excellent cooks. I've even heard of simple cooks but a natural cook … now that's a new one.
Fr Loran	*(Entering into the spirit of things)* I see what you mean. Could it be that cooking comes natural to her, that she is a sort of genius at it? *(Uses hand to explain)* Jack Dempsey was a natural fighter and … take Caruso … he was a natural singer, sure Jack Doyle was both. Say a fellow goes out and plays golf for the first time and doesn't miss the ball the first swing … well he's natural. *(There is a sobering cough from Canon Pratt, curates are attentive at once)* Sorry canon.
Fr Brest	*(To Miss Andover)* Now Miss Andover I would like to submit you to a small test.
	(Miss Andover jumps up, almost falls, recovers and sits)

Miss Andover	You won't put a hand on me. I was never touched by the hand of a man …
Fr Brest	It's not a physical test. I'll merely mention a particular word or group of words and you say whatever comes into your mind. Do you understand?
Miss Andover	All right. I'll chance it.
Fr Brest	Wardrobe!
Miss Andover	Bottle of gin!
Fr Brest	Sweet tooth!
Miss Andover	Porter cake!
Fr Brest	Sunday morning!
Miss Andover	Gin and tonic!
Fr Brest	Cold in the nose!
Miss Andover	Bloody Mary!
Canon Pratt	Sacristy!
Miss Andover	Altar wine!
	(All three exchange knowing looks)
Fr Brest	Thank you Miss Andover. We know all we need to know. You'll be hearing from us. (*Exit Miss Andover. Canon Pratt produces a pipe which he proceeds to light. Fr Brest rises and lights a cigarette. Fr Loran reads through a file)* There's a right wan!
Canon Pratt	The standard's dropped. Good housekeepers are not to be had.
Fr Brest	You must remember there's plenty of work in factories and hotels.
Canon Pratt	They don't seem anxious to make a career out of it any more. When I was a young man it was a great temptation to widows and spoiled nuns and the likes … but now they prefer the outside.

Fr Brest	But they can have the outside morning, noon and night. A parish priest's housekeeper isn't the same as a nun.
Canon Pratt	*(Thoughtfully)* They used to be. They used to be very like them in manner and in obedience. *(To Brest)* By the way you were on the ball about the drinking.
Fr Brest	I knew her late employer, Fr Dick Hennessy. Dineaway Dick the teachers of the parish used to call him.
Canon Pratt	Why Dineaway?
Fr Brest	Don't you see? He never dined at home.
Canon Pratt	Why didn't he say as much in the reference?
Fr Brest	He couldn't.
Canon Pratt	Why couldn't he?
Fr Brest	Because he wasn't able. The Lord have mercy on the poor man he could never bring himself to say a hard word about anyone.
Canon Pratt	That's why you questioned her about the drink?
Fr Brest	Of course. You may be sure if Dick Hennessy said she took a drink on occasion what he really meant was that she was a cross between a wine-taster and a dipsomaniac.
Canon Pratt	And this business about her being a natural cook?
Fr Brest	That she served up the food natural, that is to say she did not bother much with the cooking of it beforehand.
Canon Pratt	Ah ...
Fr Brest	Gentlemen, we're in a spot. Here we were without a trouble in the world, as united as three leaves on a shamrock, and as well disposed to each other as if we were brothers and now we are left to look out for ourselves. You'll never know the true worth of a real housekeeper

	till she's gone. Losing Miss Bottomley was like losing a mother.
Canon Pratt	*(Reverentially)* Lads, do you remember her pickled tongue? Her beef stew?
Fr Loran	Her shepherd's pie, canon!
Fr Brest	Her stuffed pork!
Fr Loran	Her colcannon, canon!
Canon Pratt	Jasus what she couldn't do with a duck! And lads do you remember her cockle and mussel soup? The smell of it, the taste of it. *(They fall silent, basking in the memory of such culinary delights)* This is torture lads, sheer torture. Where were we?
Fr Loran	*(Holding up a file)* This is the last one.
Canon Pratt	Who is she? Refresh me Joe, will you, like a good man.
Fr Loran	Miss Mollie Kettle age forty-seven.
Fr Brest	Forty-seven, my arse.
Canon Pratt	Well we'll soon find out when we see her. *(To Loran)* Go on father.
Fr Loran	Aged forty-seven. Worked as housekeeper in a boys' school in Liverpool, in an old folks' home in Dublin. Worked for nine years as a housekeeper to Monsignor Patrick MacMerrigan. Now retired. She's been idle for three months.
Canon Pratt	Read MacMerrigan's reference. Biggest windbag in the diocese.
Fr Loran	*(Locates and reads)* 'Miss Maureen (Mollie) Kettle', the Mollie is in brackets, 'came to work for me on the death of my housekeeper Mrs Sarah O'Hara nine years ago on the precise morning of the two thousandth and twentieth anniversary of the battle of

Pharsalia. *Quanti est sapere.* She struck me at once as being a woman of integrity. She answered all of my questions satisfactorily and having assured myself that her references were in order and that she had a reasonable knowledge of the True Faith I employed her forthwith. I found her to be a thrifty and exact housekeeper, a good time-keeper and a faithful servant. I found her to be a good cook and a better punch-maker. I know no more of the good woman nor do I need to. *Omne ignotum pro magnifico.'* *(Fr Loran puts letter aside)* That's the lot.

Fr Brest	You were right canon. He is a windbag.
Canon Pratt	To use a golfing metaphor you will understand Phil, if she could endure Monsignor MacMerrigan for nine holes, she will go the full eighteen with me.
Fr Brest	This must be approached coldly. *(Moves to centre of table)* If we lose detachment all we gain is a poor housekeeper.
Canon Pratt	Of course. Of course. Call her in Joe, like a good man, will you? *(Fr Loran rises and goes to door from where he calls)*
Fr Loran	Miss Kettle, will you please come in?
	(He returns to his former position as do others. Enter Moll Kettle. Middle-aged. Wears hat and coat, carries handbag)
Fr Brest	*(Indicates chair vacated by Miss Andover)* Please be seated.
	(Moll takes a seat and waits, smiling serenely in all directions. Coughs) Well now. It's a nice day out Miss Kettle, isn't it?
Moll	It is, thanks be to God, a very nice day entirely canon.
Canon Pratt	Allow me to introduce my two curates, Fr Brest and

	Fr Loran. It's possible they may want to ask a question or two but be at your ease, be at your ease. This isn't an inquisition. I see here that you seem to have met with Monsignor MacMerrigan's approval.
Moll	We got on great.
Fr Brest	And the new monsignor?
Moll	I couldn't tell you nothing about him father.
Fr Brest	Isn't it a wonder now you didn't stay on with him?
Moll	He didn't ask me father.
Fr Brest	And why not?
Moll	He brought his own woman with him father.
Fr Brest	You haven't worked for three months. Isn't that a long time to be without a job?
Moll	'Tis indeed father, a long time surely.
Fr Brest	Is it how you couldn't get a job?
Moll	I could get a job all right.
Fr Brest	And why didn't you take one?
Moll	After working nine years with a monsignor 'tisn't every job I *would* take. I couldn't bring myself to work with no less than a canon. 'Twould be a great come-down to me after all my years to have to fall into work with an ordinary priest.
Fr Brest	*(Looks to others for approval, laughs)* That's a very odd reason!
Canon Pratt	I don't know. I don't see anything odd about it.
Moll	'Tis hard canon, to come back to the plain black and white when one is used to the purple. Meaning no offence ….
Canon Pratt	No indeed. No indeed. And tell me now Miss Kettle, would you need help? What I mean is would you need

	an assistant?
Moll	An assistant canon?
Canon Pratt	A maidservant to help you.
Moll	I wouldn't leave one of 'em inside the door. A maidservant with curates in the house! We'll leave well enough alone canon.
Canon Pratt	How right you are Miss Kettle. What sort of a wage would you be expecting?
Moll	Eight pounds a week canon, and if we didn't fall out you might see your way to giving me a rise after a year or two.
Canon Pratt	I might so. I might so.
Fr Brest	Have you any hobbies?
Moll	Bingo father. Only on the Sunday night, and the television now and then.
Fr Brest	The disease of bingo: I see faith. Well we haven't been invaded by that particular malady in this parish yet and if I have my way we never will.
Fr Loran	Might I ask a question?
Canon Pratt	I suppose so.
Fr Loran	What do you think of Vatican Two?
Moll	What's that father?
Fr Loran	Vatican Two. What do you think of it?
Moll	Hawaii–Five–O is my own favourite father.
Canon Pratt	Now, now father. You mustn't expect the good woman to know about these things. Tell me Miss Kettle, when could you begin work … that is if we decided to take you on?
Moll	I could come in the morning canon.
Canon Pratt	I see. Well lads, any more questions?

Fr Brest	I presume Monsignor MacMerrigan had curates.
Moll	He had father, three of 'em.
Fr Brest	And did you get references from those?
Moll	I did not indeed.
Fr Brest	And why not?
Moll	No one takes notice of a curate's reference father.
Fr Brest	Huh?
Fr Loran	Nobody!
Moll	Well nobody except another curate.
	(The canon seems to enjoy this)
Fr Brest	No more questions.
Canon Pratt	Very well then. Miss Kettle would you be good enough to wait outside for a few minutes? I assure you we won't keep you long. *(Moll takes handbag, folds arms and exits. The canon rises and stands with his back to fireplace)* Now's the time to say it lads.
Fr Brest	I don't know ....
Canon Pratt	What don't you know?
Fr Brest	There's something about her.
Fr Loran	I think she's all right. She's not very bright but she's all right.
Fr Brest	*(Rises and paces)* Now that's where I disagree entirely with you. You say she's not very bright I say otherwise. She may give the impression that she's not bright but I say she's a lot sharper than she lets on to be.
Canon Pratt	And what if she is? So long as she fits the bill what else matters? I may tell you Phil, that I think we would be danged lucky to have her.
Fr Loran	I agree
Canon Pratt	Come on Phil, make it unanimous.

Fr Brest	I wish I could. This woman frightens me. There's something hidden beneath that calm surface. She's too quick with her answers.
Fr Loran	Now Phil …
Fr Brest	No Joe. I'm seriously concerned. When a presbytery gets a new housekeeper it's like a regiment that gets a new sergeant major. A new housekeeper is like a new moon and a new moon can bring anything from a tidal wave to an earthquake.
Canon Pratt	You're an alarmist Phil.
Fr Brest	Maybe but I have a foreboding. In these matters I'm as sensitive as a seismograph.
Fr Loran	A what?
Fr Brest	Seismograph!
Fr Loran	Oh, yes.
Fr Brest	And already I am recording the first faint vibrations of a calamity that is about to befall. I am registering the first awful rumblings of a collapsing presbytery. *(Others laugh, Fr Brest sits)*
Canon Pratt	Spare the flowery language for Sunday's sermon father.
Fr Brest	All right but don't forget I warned you.
Canon Pratt	Are we agreed then?
Others	Agreed.
Canon Pratt	I'm glad that we're decided. I think we chose wisely. *(Canon moves to the door)* Miss Kettle, will you come in please? *(Moll enters)* Will you be good enough to take a seat Miss Kettle? *(Moll sits)* Your Christian name is Maureen, is it not?
Moll	That's right canon although them that knows me calls

17

	me 'Moll'.
Canon Pratt	'Moll' is it? Well now Moll, we have good news for you girl. Whenever you're ready you can begin work. The salary is agreed. I'm sorry it's not more but we are a very poor parish with a new school to be built and repairs to the church and God knows what else.
Moll	'Tis all right canon. I'm sure I'll manage – as I've always done.
Canon Pratt	I dare say we might agree that a month's notice either way would be reasonable, in case things don't work out.
Moll	Ah, they'll work out fine canon, you'll see.
Canon Pratt	Very well then. If you'll come with me I'll show you the layout of the place *(Canon rises and indicates other exit. Moll rises)*
Moll	*(To all)* I hope now please God that it will be the lucky day for all of us.
Canon Pratt	Yes, please God.
Fr Loran	Please God.
Canon Pratt	Of course we have a handy man and then there's the parish clerk and as you say … *(Exit Moll and canon)*
Fr Loran	For better or for worse we have ourselves a housekeeper. *(Collects papers)*
Fr Brest	I've said my piece. Only time can tell. I hope for your sake and mine I'm proved wrong.
Fr Loran	I think you're being ridiculous, now, you know. *(Crosses to fireplace, puts papers away on top of pouffe there)*
Fr Brest	Remember that I am a veteran of five presbyteries and I happen to know that God's greatest blessing is a good housekeeper but that God's greatest curse is a

bad one. I haven't met a bad one yet but I know men who have. They died from malnutrition. This woman strikes me as a bad one. I could be wrong but I feel it in my bones and my bones have yet to let me down. I have to go. I'll see you later. *(Moves to door down left)*

Fr Loran   Where are you going?

Fr Brest   I'm going for a round of golf if you must know but first I'm going out to the chapel and in the chapel I propose to go down on my two knees and commence a novena for the salvation of all of us, not to any saint and not to any martyr but straight through, no messing and no diversions, straight through to God the Father Almighty Himself. Be seein' you.

(Exits)

BRIDGE ACT ONE, SCENE ONE TO SCENE TWO

Canon Pratt   Of the many afflictions that annoy the human condition the poisonous canker of Doubt seems to me one of the most potent and least recognised. And Doubt has an insidious and deadly effect upon the infected person bringing torment to the soul and encouraging a terrible railing against the will of God, erupting in fits of rage.

For my part I thank God for the blessing of Optimism. And my faith in Optimism was never better justified than in the case of Moll Kettle for when I offered the opinion that we had chosen wisely in appointing her as our housekeeper my words were clearly divinely inspired ...

Action takes place as before. The time is morning, a month later. The priests and canon are seated at table breakfasting. The canon is eating heartily, Fr Loran not so heartily and Fr Brest not at all. Moll enters with bowl of black and white pudding.

Moll   Excuse me canon. *(Loads canon's plate)*

Canon Pratt   Watch out, I'll burst.

Moll   Just a little more. Is the breakfast all right canon?

Canon Pratt   Fine, fine, couldn't be better. How long are you with us now Moll?

Moll   A month yesterday canon.

Canon Pratt   *(Heartily)* A month yesterday, faith. Well, now does time be long in passing? Off with you Moll. We're fine here.

Moll	Thank you canon. *(Is about to exit)* What about the dinner canon?
Canon Pratt	We'll leave that entirely to yourself Moll.
Moll	Would bacon and turnips be all right then?
Canon Pratt	Bacon and turnips would be glorious Moll, just glorious.
Moll	Thank you canon. *(Exits)*
Canon Pratt	There's a great woman.
Fr Brest	I don't know all about that.
Canon Pratt	*(Still eating away heartily)* You haven't hit it off with her Phil, have you?
Fr Brest	Quite frankly, no.
Canon Pratt	Well we mustn't let it spoil our breakfast.

(Canon resumes eating. Fr Loran nibbles. Fr Brest does not eat but with his knife probes through objects on his plate. He frowns. He bends over plate, exaggeratedly peering at contents, finally he lifts up a tiny object. He holds it in front of him)

Fr Brest	Fr Loran?
Fr Loran	Yes Fr Brest.
Fr Brest	You're a man who has excellent eye-sight.
Fr Loran	Well, I don't need spectacles anyway, thanks be to God.
Fr Brest	That's good. Perhaps you could tell me what this is which I am holding in my hand. Take your time now … *(Fr Loran looks carefully at object and shakes his head)*
Fr Loran	It beats me.
Fr Brest	Does it remind you of anything?

Fr Loran	Offhand I can't say.
Fr Brest	Here take it in your hand and make a careful examination. *(Fr Loran accepts object and turns it over in his hand)* Interesting, isn't it?
Fr Loran	It certainly is. I must confess I'm baffled. *(Holds it out in front of him)* I honestly can't say what it is.
Fr Brest	Have you ever seen anything like it before?
Fr Loran	*(More examination)* N … No. I can't say that I have.
Fr Brest	Hand it back, please. It could be valuable.
Fr Loran	Valuable?
Fr Brest	Museums and universities are always interested in curiosities.
Canon Pratt	*(Crossly)* Do I detect a note of sarcasm Fr Brest, because if I do I may tell you here and now I won't have it. What in blazes are you on about then?
Fr Brest	*(Exhibits rasher)* It's this.
Canon Pratt	*(Suspiciously)* What is it?
Fr Brest	I wish I knew.
	(The canon peers closely at it)
Canon Pratt	Damn and blast it man, that's a rasher.
Fr Brest	Is it?
Canon Pratt	It is of course.
Fr Brest	But it's too small to be a rasher.
Canon Pratt	It's still a rasher.
Fr Brest	*(Irked)* It must have come off a bloody banbh.
Fr Loran	Or a pyg … my.
Canon Pratt	What?
Fr Loran	Get it, a pygmy, hah?
Canon Pratt	*(Conciliatory)* Come on Phil. Stop the nonsense and eat your breakfast, like a good boy.

Fr Brest	What breakfast?
Canon Pratt	The breakfast on your plate. I see nothing wrong with it.
Fr Brest	What you mean is there's nothing wrong with yours. You did all right for yourself. Look at the size of your sausages and look at the size of ours. *(He holds up a sausage)* What do you think of that?
Fr Loran	Normal sausages run about sixteen to the pound. Forty-eight of these wouldn't make a pound. Of course I don't mind. I haven't much of an appetite anyway but it's tough on poor Phil canon.
Fr Brest	You're bloody sure it's tough on poor Phil.
Canon Pratt	Maybe they are what are known as cocktail sausages. It's a fact you know that there could be more nourishment in a small meaty, hardy sort of a sausage than you'd get out of a big, fat, soft one.
Fr Brest	*(Sarcastically)* Is that a fact?
Canon Pratt	Oh, yes indeed. Isn't there a saying to cover it, what in blazes is it again … something to do with parcels.
Fr Loran	The best of goods come in small parcels.
Canon Pratt	That's the one. Good man Joe. There's a lot to some of these old sayings, you know.
Fr Brest	Fair enough then I'll tell you what we'll do. In future you can have the small hardy sausages and I'll take the big, fat ones.
Canon Pratt	What's gotten into you lately Phil?
Fr Brest	It's the housekeeper, your precious Moll. She seems to think the curates can live on the wind.
Canon Pratt	Now, now the poor woman does the best she can.
Fr Brest	She does the best she can for you.

Canon Pratt	That's your imagination.
Fr Brest	Is it ...? *(Sticks a fork in the canon's remaining sausage. Sticks fork in one of his own sausages)* Have a look canon. Now is it my imagination? Am I seeing things canon, or is one of those sausages three times as large as the other? Am I seeing things Fr Loran?
Fr Loran	You are *not*.
Fr Brest	Am I canon ...?
Canon Pratt	If you want fat sausages why in blazes don't you ask for fat sausages?
Fr Brest	*(Returning sausages)* All right, I'm asking for them now.
Canon Pratt	*(Coldly)* Very good. You've made your point. May we proceed with our breakfasts?
Fr Brest	You proceed by all means but I have something more to say.
Canon Pratt	*(Eating calmly)* You'd better get it off your chest then, hadn't you?
Fr Brest	Yes. I had better hadn't I? *(Fr Brest rises. Fr Loran would caution him to use restraint but Brest has the floor)* That woman in there, that so-called housekeeper has deliberately gone out of her way to make my life a misery since she came here a month ago. I was an easy-going placid man, a happy man in a happy house, content with my fare and with my lot and then slowly, insidiously, poisonously she tries to break me ...
Canon Pratt	What a vivid imagination you have Phil.
Fr Brest	Have I? Have you heard her when she calls me? I'm relaxed and happy and then suddenly in the distance I hear the shriek ... *(Imitates shrill, shrieking voice)* 'Fr

	Brest, Fr Breest', I tell you I'm shattered.
Canon Pratt	For God's sake Phil, gather hold of yourself. The poor woman has nothing against you.
Fr Brest	Hasn't she? Did I hear you agree to bacon and turnips for lunch today …?
Canon Pratt	Yes … but we can always change it if you want to …
Fr Brest	I know what I'll get today. I'll get the stringiest, toughest, smallest piece of the whole lot. Something leathery and lardy from the middle of an old sow's belly.
Fr Loran	So will I.
Fr Brest	*(To Loran angrily)* Yes, but you have no appetite and I have. *(To canon)* You watch it now at lunchtime … just see for yourself if I'm exaggerating … in the interests of common justice have a look at my plate.
Canon Pratt	Why don't you have a talk with her?
Fr Brest	I would never demean myself by talking with a creature like that.
Canon Pratt	Oh, dear me, we're very perturbed this morning.
Fr Brest	*(Spreading hands out for calm and reasoning)* All right. You remember yesterday's lunch?
Canon Pratt	*(Reluctantly)* Yes.
Fr Brest	What did it consist of?
Canon Pratt	I have an atrocious memory.
Fr Brest	I'll help you. Were there some lamb chops?
Canon Pratt	I believe there were some lamb chops.
Fr Brest	The exact number canon?
Canon Pratt	I think there were three.
Fr Brest	So there were three. Good. May I ask what else was on the plate?

Canon Pratt	*(Thoughtfully)* Peas I believe. Yes, I'm certain there were some peas.
Fr Brest	How many peas?
Canon Pratt	*(Laughs)* Oh, now Phil, I didn't count them ...
Fr Brest	Of course you didn't. As I recall you had a very large plate. In fact I would not be wrong if I said that it was more of a dish than a plate ...
Canon Pratt	*(Irritation)* Go on. Go on.
Fr Brest	Half the dish was taken up by the three lamb cutlets. What my dear canon, took up the rest of the area of the plate?
Canon Pratt	*(Sighs)* Peas I said but what's the point father?
Fr Brest	So we may presume that an area of almost one square foot was entirely covered by peas. How many peas would you say there were in this area of the plate?
Canon Pratt	*(Severely)* All right, there were a few hundred peas or thereabouts. I can't be certain.
Fr Brest	Thank you canon. You have been most helpful. Now did you see what was on my plate canon?
Canon Pratt	No. I did not. I had something better to do.
Fr Brest	Oh begob, you had! What was on my plate Fr Loran? And please speak up. *(Loran tries to speak but Brest flows on)* I want you to be heard. Now what was on my plate father?
Fr Loran	*(Entering into the spirit of the thing)* There was what appeared to be one small mutton chop or some article which outwardly resembled a small mutton chop. It was, if I may say so, the smallest mutton chop I have ever seen ...
Fr Brest	Go on please. What else father?

Fr Loran	There also appeared to be a small quantity of what seemed to me to be tinned peas.
Fr Brest	Could we be a little bit more specific father? Take your time but be honest in your answer.
Fr Loran	It is my honest opinion that there were twenty peas on the plate.
Fr Brest	You are wrong father. I counted those peas and instead of twenty there were nineteen peas. Is this fair canon? Is this honest canon?
Canon Pratt	I'll talk to her. I had no hand in it I assure you. I'll talk to her this very day.
Fr Brest	I believe you but before I close let me add that I could not chew the meat of that chop yesterday. I tried and failed. I hacked at it and I tore at it but I made no impression. I can only conclude that the same chop which I euphemistically called mutton was not mutton at all. *(Goes furiously towards exit where he stands)* I can only conclude that it was hacked, gartered and hewn from the posterior of a mountain ram who was siring ewes when Holy St Patrick was a boy in the mountains of Antrim. *(Exits)*
Canon Pratt	By the Lord but that was a mighty outburst Joe.
Fr Loran	He's been complaining with a bit.
Canon Pratt	That's the first I heard.
Fr Loran	I suppose he kept it in for too long, hence the unexpected explosion.
Canon Pratt	And do you agree with him?
Fr Loran	Well, I do and I don't.
Canon Pratt	Well, do you or don't you?
Fr Loran	Well, I think I do but on the other hand ….

Canon Pratt	I'll have a talk with her.
	(In the distance can be heard the high pitched sound of Moll's voice calling Fr Brest)
Fr Loran	No time like the present. Here she comes. I'll skedaddle. *(Enter Moll)*
Moll	Where's Fr Brest?
Canon Pratt	Who wants him?
Moll	There's a sick call.
Fr Loran	I'll take it Miss Kettle.
Moll	Very well. The man is waiting outside.
Fr Loran	The ball is at your feet canon. Watch how you kick. *(Exits)*
Canon Pratt	Moll will you sit down for a minute? I want to have a little talk with you.
Moll	Very good canon. *(Moll takes a seat)*
Canon Pratt	Moll ... poor Fr Brest is very perturbed.
Moll	Oh the poor man, I hope he'll get out of it!
Canon Pratt	He thinks you're cutting down on his food. So does Fr Loran but Loran doesn't seem to mind.
Moll	Enough is enough canon and I've always given the pair of them enough. Maybe 'tis how they expect the same as yourself.
Canon Pratt	That's just it Moll. They do and they have every right to expect it.
Moll	Have they no respect for seniority?
Canon Pratt	All I know is that Fr Brest maintains he is not getting enough to eat. Now what have you to say to that?
Moll	Your last housekeeper canon, spent forty pounds a month on meat alone for this household. That much money would keep a company of soldiers in meat.

	Forty pounds on meat alone.
Canon Pratt	Was it that much?
Moll	Every penny of it canon.
Canon Pratt	And how much was it this month Moll?
Moll	Ten pounds canon.
Canon Pratt	Great God Moll but you're a pure magician. And the food was never better. *(Corrects himself)* My food was never better. And did you cut down much on the other items Moll?
Moll	I did indeed canon. The grocery bill is cut by half.
Canon Pratt	Great God but you're a genius entirely Moll. Still we have this problem about Fr Brest.
Moll	God save us all canon but 'tis wrong to give young priests too much to eat.
Canon Pratt	Why would you say that Moll?
Moll	Because they gets notions canon.
Canon Pratt	Notions Moll?
Moll	Notions canon. Over in Scotland canon a few years ago a young curate rose up one morning without his collar and went off with a half-naked lady acrobat.
Canon Pratt	Ah, go on …
Moll	A lady acrobat. 'Twas in the papers canon. Beef canon, and steaks that was half raw was the cause of it. That was what Monsignor MacMerrigan's doctor told us. He knew the curate. If 'twas plain bread and butter and gravy he was getting he'd be too weak to get notions.
Canon Pratt	I dare say there's something in what you say Moll.
Moll	In the name of God canon, will you look at the jaunty cut of them two hardy bucks.

Canon Pratt	Ah, now they're young and they're …
Moll	Isn't that what I'm at canon?
Canon Pratt	Huh?
Moll	Two prime bucks and they have the gall to look for more food. Sure if they eat any more they'll go out of their minds altogether. If you feed them like game-cocks they'll crow like gamecocks and they'll strut like gamecocks.
Canon Pratt	And you think they're getting enough?
Moll	Are they priests or are they gluttons canon? Is there nothing else to life but their gullets? Would you hear the pope asking for lamb cutlets? When Cardinal Monsooki from Persia came to see the monsignor two years ago, did he ask for lamb cutlets? He did not indeed. A plate of giblet soup and a crust of bread was all the poor man had and he a cardinal. Yet we have two pampered bucks looking for lamb cutlets, begrudging their own canon the bite he does be eating. What worries have them two beyond the filling of their bellies? Have they to think about the education of children and the building of schools or is their guts their only concern?
Canon Pratt	I can't answer you Moll. In all truth Moll, I can't answer you.
Moll	*(She rises and starts to tidy table)* And will you tell me another thing canon?
Canon Pratt	I will if I can Moll.
Moll	The church canon. There's three holes in the roof, canon, and the windows are rotten. Are the people of the parish canon, to be exposed to rain and cold and draughts

because Fr Brest don't like bingo?

Canon Pratt The people of the parish must come before all else Moll, before me, you, before anybody.

Moll Would you like to see the old people catching pneumonia when they kneel down to say their prayers? Is that what you want canon? Is it how you want the feeble and the delicate to be bent over with pain, and them that has weak joints to be crippled?

Canon Pratt 'Tis not what I want Moll.

Moll We'll be all racked with pleurisy and T.B. if them holes in the roof aren't seen to. And why canon? Will you tell me why?

Canon Pratt Because Fr Brest doesn't like bingo.

Moll And does he like bridge canon?

Canon Pratt By all accounts he's a dab hand at it Moll.

Moll And golf canon. Don't he play golf?

Canon Pratt He plays golf. In fact he has won tournaments Moll.

Moll So 'tis all right for Fr Brest and his equals to play golf and bridge.

Canon Pratt Yes. 'Tis all right for them.

Moll *(About to exit with hands full of breakfast things)* But 'tis not all right for the poor people of this parish to play an innocent game of bingo.

(Enter Brest in a hurry)

Fr Brest Well did you have a talk with Moll about the food?

Canon Pratt Indeed I did – we're putting a new roof on the church.

Fr Brest What's that got to do with it – where are you going to get the money?

Canon Pratt   You're going to get it Fr Brest. From now on you're in charge of the bingo.

(Moll laughs and exits)

BRIDGE ACT ONE, SCENE TWO TO SCENE THREE

Canon Pratt   If there is a sound that pleases me more than most 'tis the sound of laughter. Laughter erupts from the soul in an irrepressible declamation of an excess of good humour.

Laughter is natural, you see. 'Tis one of the many magical gifts the good Lord provides. The warmth of the sun, the whisper of the trees, the murmur of the sea. The nectar of the very air we breathe. Go right ahead, says the Lord. 'Tis free. Enjoy it.

The time is evening of a day several months after the arrival of Moll Kettle. Moll is dusting. As she dusts the several chairs they bring to her mind her impressions of the three who normally sit in them. Then she goes to dust a picture behind the door down left and while she is there the two curates burst in, concealing her behind it.

Fr Brest   We made it. *(Shakes Loran's hand)* Congratulations *(Loran puzzled)* on evading you know who. I'll ring the mother while I have the chance. She's taken to listening in on telephone calls now. *(Picks up the phone to dial)* The other night I was on to her and in the middle of the conversation I sensed there was someone in the vicinity. *(Puts down phone)*

Fr Loran   And was she there?

Fr Brest   She was standing behind the door of this very room. *(With his back to it slams the door. Loran sees Moll, but*

	Brest doesn't) Still as a statue, hardly breathing, with an innocent look on her face as if she weren't listening at all. *(Loran gestures, Brest turns and sees Moll)* What are you doing there?
Moll	Doing where boybawn?
Fr Brest	Doing there; hiding behind the door.
Moll	Cobwebs, I'm hunting cobwebs. The presbytery is draped with them.
Fr Brest	Do you realise that I was making a phone call to my mother? You were eavesdropping again, you ought to be ashamed of yourself. Would you mind leaving the room now so that I can ring my mother?
Moll	I'll go boybawn when I have the cobwebs cleared.
Fr Brest	You'll go now!
Moll	I was here before you.
Fr Brest	If you don't leave this room instantly I will remove you forcibly.
Fr Loran	Keep your temper! No violence.
Moll	I'm going to say a rosary for the poor souls – but remember one thing …
Fr Brest	What would that be?
Moll	A call to your mother is not church business.
Fr Brest	Meaning what?
Moll	Meaning that you can leave the money for the call beside the phone. *(She exits in triumph)*
Fr Loran	Well, mother love is a wonderful thing – but it will cost you money from now on.
Fr Brest	May God forgive me but I can't bear that woman. *(On phone)* Get me Castletownbere 49.
Fr Loran	*(Putting his coat and hat on small table up-stage)* We are

	supposed to show meekness and sufferance in the face of adversity. Our first function is forbearance.
Fr Brest	It's me or she and by the Lord Heavens it's not going to be me … no, no miss, not you … I mean it's going to be me or she … all right, ring me back *(Puts down phone)*
Fr Loran	Well, what was it you were going to tell me?
Fr Brest	*(Tossing down a letter)* What do you think of that?
Fr Loran	What is it?
Fr Brest	Take a look.
Fr Loran	*(Reluctantly takes out the letter)* You wrote to Monsignor MacMerrigan!
Fr Brest	I did.
Fr Loran	*(Reading)* He's in rare form all right … 'let me say that you have an irrational impertinence which will land you in hot water some day. So you want further information about Moll Kettle. If you must know she was a great woman entirely. She ran the presbytery on a pittance and if there were more like her there wouldn't be half the trouble in the Church today. You are an impatient and ungodly fellow to want to belittle this woman. Prayer is the last hope for you, prayer and meditation. I need not add fasting because Moll Kettle will see to that. Ha. Ha. May God succour you father and your many Godless equals. The Church is at the crossroads. Make sure you follow the right path. Yours in J. C. Monsignor Patrick MacMerrigan.' *(Returns the letter)*
Fr Brest	How did an old bags like that come to be a monsignor?
Fr Loran	Probably fit for nothing else.

Fr Brest	I also wrote to two of his curates.
Fr Loran	I thought there were three.
Fr Brest	There were but one died shortly after Moll left.
Fr Loran	From what?
Fr Brest	From a mixture of maleficence, malnutrition and pernicious anaemia.
Fr Loran	That last one. What is it?
Fr Brest	It's what you and I will die from if we don't get to her first.
Fr Loran	That's nice. Did you get replies to those letters?
Fr Brest	I did.
Fr Loran	Show us. *(Brest is about to hand over both, but on second thoughts retains one and reads it out himself)*
Fr Brest	This is from Fr Paddy O'Shaughnessy who was the senior curate in Moll's early time with MacMerrigan. *(Reads)* 'Dear Phil, Good to hear from you. Saw where you won the West Cork fourball. Congrats. I heard a great night was had by all and you had to be carried … *(Brest stops and edits the next section of the letter)* About our friend to whom I will not refer by name as I would put nothing past her, not even the steaming open of this letter…'
Fr Loran	I don't doubt him. I don't doubt him one bit.
Fr Brest	Quiet … *(Reads)* 'I am, as you know from our student days, a more than passable linguist. In point of fact I now speak four languages fluently. I have a fair knowledge of seven others but in the entire eleven there is no word or group of words which would adequately describe the demon in your midst. Cunning, sharp, deadly, evil itself personified. In the early days of the human

species before language was needed she would have been eliminated by what bookmakers refer to as tick-tack. My current choice of foods is grossly restricted from the beating she gave my stomach. You know me Phil. We got on, you and I, but lest there be any doubt in your mind about you know who remember Fr Paul Mannick, our dear departed colleague.'

Fr Loran	Is that the third one?
Fr Brest	Yes.
Fr Loran	Requiescat in Pace.
Fr Brest	'If he could shed the boards and the brown cloths that bind him and rise from the grave he would point a bony finger in the direction of a certain woman whose name is known to all of us. I conclude. Yours fondly, Fr Paddy O'Shaughnessy. P.S. In the honour of God either burn or ate this epistle.'
Fr Loran	Cogent.
Fr Brest	Most cogent.
Fr Loran	Tells its own tale.
Fr Brest	Forcibly.
Fr Loran	Agreed.
Fr Brest	*(Proudly)* However that last letter from the middle curate as he styles himself, tells all succinctly and savagely.
Fr Loran	*(Reading)* 'Dear Fr Brest, I am only the middle curate. You should not involve me. I am neither craven nor cowardly but remember that she who is your housekeeper today could be mine tomorrow. *(Look of alarm at Brest)* For this reason, I am afraid to say more but I'll put it this way. If I were sending a telegram it

would say "abandon ship". Sincerely, Robert Connors, C.C.' *(Returns letter)*

Fr Brest   Paints a strange picture, does it not?

Fr Loran   Weird. What are we going to do?

Fr Brest   There's only one thing we can do.

Fr Loran   What's that?

Fr Brest   The bishop.

Fr Loran   You mean a visit?

Fr Brest   Not necessarily, a confidential letter would do.

Fr Loran   That's pretty drastic.

Fr Brest   She's been with us four months and already I have conducted fifty sessions of bingo, each lasting four hours. I have lost fifteen pounds in weight. I have become a martyr to malnutrition. It will have to be the bishop. A joint letter.

Fr Loran   Count me out.

Fr Brest   You can't opt out. We have to make a stand.

Fr Loran   It won't work.

Fr Brest   Why not?

Fr Loran   Because once you've written one letter to the bishop you can never do it again. Suppose we write to him and tell him the truth about Moll, we will forever after, in his eyes, be the two curates who complained about the food. If sometime either one of us has another complaint to make, he'll say to himself that is one of the two who complained before. You get it?

Fr Brest   No. I don't get it. We have a genuine grouse.

Fr Loran   But have we? There's plenty bread and butter. There's milk and there are potatoes. No scarcity of essentials if you know what I mean. If the bishop investigates he's

38

	not going to do so without informing the canon and informing the canon, as we both know, is the same as informing Moll. She'll be ready for the bishop. Is it a woman that fobbed off Cardinal Monsooki with watery giblet soup?
Fr Brest	You won't sign then?
Fr Loran	Let's wait. If things get worse I'll reconsider. We have very little to show you know; we have no proof. Honestly, Phil, you may have lost weight but you were over-eating. You've never looked as fit. Your belly's gone. You're not flabby anymore.
Fr Brest	I'm living off my fat, I tell you, and when that runs out it's only a matter of time until the major collapse. Hush … *(To door)* what was that? *(Both men become alert and listen carefully. Brest opens door slightly, Loran comes up behind him. Both listen, Brest turns)*
Fr Loran	It sounds like the banshee to me.
Fr Brest	Worse. It's the voice of Moll Kettle. Listen …. *(Again they both listen and after a little while unmistakably Moll's voice can be heard)*
Moll	Fr Breest … where are you? … Fr Breest.
Fr Brest	There's no escape. *(Produces letters)* Let's burn this lot. *(He opens and crumbles them, helped by Fr Loran. They light the pile)*
Fr Loran	Give them to me and I'll burn them. *(At fireplace)* Here she is. *(Enter Moll)*
Moll	Fr Bree … Oh, there you are!
Fr Brest	What's the matter now?
Moll	The matter is that there's a sick call and there's no priest to take it.

Fr Brest	We're off-duty.
Moll	One of you is supposed to be on call.
Fr Brest	The canon is also a priest, you know. He was ordained too, the same as Fr Loran and myself.
Moll	The canon went to bed an hour ago with a cold in the head and I have no notion of sending him traipsing into the countryside not knowing would he catch his death of pneumonia.
Fr Brest	Where is the sick call?
Moll	Hurry on. The man is waiting at the door of the presbytery. Hurry on before some poor soul faces his maker without a priest. *(Goes out door)*
Fr Brest	There's no peace to be had any more.
Moll	*(Comes back)* Wouldn't it be nice now if the bishop heard there was no priest to take a sick call? Suppose I didn't bother searching. 'Tis not my duty you know to locate missing curates. *(Goes out)*
Fr Brest	That will do you now. Enough guff, thank you.
Moll	*(Comes back)* What's the bonfire for?
Fr Loran	Just some waste Miss Kettle. 'Tis all right.
Fr Brest	I don't see that it's any of your business.
Moll	Waste paper that had to be burned. Ha! Ha! That must have been the hot paper.
Fr Brest	If it wasn't hot before it's hot now.
Moll	*(About to exit)* You'd better hurry and don't forget the two of you are on the bingo tonight in the parish hall.
Fr Brest	Tonight is Wednesday – there's no bingo.
Moll	There's a special session tonight for the Church holiday.
Fr Brest	And I was playing golf with the doctor.

Fr Loran	And I was playing records for the reverend mother …
Moll	Well now, legs eleven, the doc can go play golf with the reverend mother; because tonight the pair of you are on the bingo. Check!

(Exits)

BRIDGE ACT ONE, SCENE THREE TO SCENE FOUR

Canon Pratt   A word about the bingo. Bingo is no sin. There are some who will tell you that bingo is gambling and that therefore bingo is a pernicious evil preying upon the vulnerability of simple people.

Yirra, bingo is not gambling at all but a harmless bit o' fun. The prizes are modest and, though welcome, unlikely to launch a winner into the perilous seas of high finance, particularly since there is every encouragement to reinvest in the parish funds for the glorification of God and the salvation of the donor's soul.

Moll at the telephone.

Moll   *(On phone)* There's none of the curates here now. *(Listens)* Oh! The canon is resting and can't be disturbed … *(Listens)* You must talk to him … a matter of life and death? Listen here to me now. Fr Loran is at choir practice. Fr Brest is in bed. I'm not going to call the canon unless there's anointing to be done. What's up with you anyway? *(Listens)* You're pregnant? Well that's hardly the fault of the canon. *(Listens)* Yes? Yes? You had a right to think of that my dear girl before you let him put the honey in your coffee. *(Listens)* A what? He gave you a green cough drop and told you 'twas the pill. You must be a right eejit. *(Puts down the phone)*

Bridgie	*(Coming in)* 'Tis me. The canon isn't in, I suppose, is he? I suppose he isn't, is he?
Moll	Weren't you one of the women in for this job?
Bridgie	That's right. No hard feelings.
Moll	What can I do for you?
Bridgie	*(Sits down)* I want to see one of the curates.
Moll	They're not here now.
Bridgie	*(Sits left of table)* The canon will do just as well.
Moll	The canon is resting.
Bridgie	Oh dear! That's a pity.
Moll	Maybe I might be able to help. I often stands in for the canon. Out with it now, whatever it is.
Bridgie	I'm thinking of getting married.
Moll	Are you in earnest?
Bridgie	Oh, I am!
Moll	And who is he?
Bridgie	*(Calls)* Ulick … Ulick love … come in and let the woman see you … *(Enter a man of advanced years, wearing a cap and long overcoat. He is the very epitome of deference. He wears strong-lensed specs)* He's very shy.
Moll	Will you sit down sir? *(He smiles and shrugs his way out of doing so)* Are you sure you want to go ahead?
Bridgie	What's wrong with him?
Moll	He'll die on the job.
Bridgie	If he do, won't I have my widow's pension!
Moll	What do you want to get married for anyway?
Bridgie	I have to.
Moll	You have to? Miracles will never cease. There's hope for us all. *(To Ulick)* Shove out here wonder-boy till I have a look at you.

Bridgie	Shove out Ulick, and let the woman have a look at you.
Moll	Are you sure he's the man?
Bridgie	He's the best I could get. I'm no chicken, you know.
Moll	Will you answer an honest question?
Bridgie	Of course.
Moll	Are you long gone?
Bridgie	Long gone where?
Moll	You know where.
Bridgie	I don't, honest I don't.
Moll	How many months?
Bridgie	What are you talking about?
Moll	You said you had to get married.
Bridgie	*(Goes into paroxysm of laughter)* Did you hear that Ulick? What she's pinning on you? Yirra get on with ya. I have to get married because I can't get a job. I spent my life working for priests and here I am penniless in the end.
Moll	God knows 'tis true. And did you save anything?
Bridgie	Save on what a priest would pay? You must be mad. The same thing will happen to you some day unless you look out for yourself.
Moll	*(Thoughtfully)* There's a lot to what you say. You've put me thinking, God knows.
Bridgie	How much to get married anyway?
Moll	Two pounds a cow, ten shillings a bullock, five bob a sheep, two bob a goat and a shilling a pig.
Bridgie	How many cows have you Ulick? *(Ulick lifts four fingers of left hand and holds up other hand clenched)* Four cows and a bull.

Moll	Eight pounds. Yerra give me a forty quid and I'll come round the canon. You gave me good advice. If I don't look out for myself the canon won't.
Bridgie	Have you forty handy Ulick? *(Ulick locates purse and extracts money, Bridgie takes it and hands it to Moll, who accepts it)*
Moll	Let the two of you be here next Monday morning at eight o'clock. *(Moll listens to noise outside)* Go on now. Off ye go.
Bridgie	I'll be looking forward to it, and pray that I'll be guided right. *(Exit Bridgie)*
Moll	Ulick? *(Ulick pauses)* Take it nice and easy at the start. If you get over the first fence without a fall you'll finish the course no bother.
Ulick	There's no fear of a fall. I'd say she was often saddled before. *(Exit Ulick)*

END OF ACT ONE

ACT TWO

SCENE ONE

Action takes place in the dining cum sitting-room of the presbytery. The canon is sitting in a comfortable chair near the fire, while Moll arranges table for supper. The canon smokes his pipe. In the distance can be heard the voices of men and women singing the Adoremus …

Moll	I can put up the supper any time canon.
Canon Pratt	We'll wait Moll, till Fr Loran is finished with the choir practice. That was a great idea of yours to get a choir going.
Moll	Thank you canon.
Canon Pratt	Do you like hymns Moll?
Moll	I do canon, but hymns are sad.
Canon Pratt	That's just the way Fr Loran's choir sings them. How long are you here now Moll?
Moll	*(Laying table)* Gone the twelve months canon.
Canon Pratt	Gone the twelve months. That bingo was a great idea too. The bare year gone by and the church is repaired, the foundations for the school are dug and work will start next week. I never thought I'd live to see the day. The bishop is your happy man. Did I tell you he complimented me on the fundraising?
Moll	Did he now?
Canon Pratt	He told me I was a credit to the diocese. I'm very mindful, said he, of good builders and I'm very

	thankful, said he, to priests who build modern schools. I often think of them, he said.
Moll	*(Repeats)* He often think of them. What did he mean by that, I wonder?
Canon Pratt	You never know till after what a bishop means Moll, as many a poor priest knows to his cost. All we can do is hope for the best. Still and all, the outlook is good and God is good too.
Moll	God knows but 'tis fine for you. 'Tis how you'll wind up bishop one day yourself.
Canon Pratt	Doubtful Moll, but men were made monsignors with far less to their credit.
Moll	'Tis fine for some.
Canon Pratt	*(Looks at her suspiciously)* Am I right in thinking we have a touch of the sulks today …? Come on Moll. You know me. Out with it, whatever it is.
Moll	I don't know should I canon.
Canon Pratt	Sit down Moll. *(Moll takes a seat)* Now let's have it. 'Tis always better to get a thing out. And you know me … It won't pass my lips whatever it is. You may talk to me in complete confidence.
Moll	'Tis money canon.
Canon Pratt	There are other things in the world besides money girl. There is the grace of God which is more important than all the wealth and all the riches of the five continents put together.
Moll	True for you canon but couldn't a person have the grace of God and have a bit of money beside it?
Canon Pratt	Spell it out to me Moll.
Moll	I won't put a tooth in it canon. Security, my own

	security has me worried sick. I'm getting old canon and you're not getting any younger yourself so 'tis time I thought about what I would do should anything happen to you. I'd be worse off than a widow.
Canon Pratt	Worse than a widow?
Moll	She would have her widow's pension. I wouldn't have a copper to get from anyone. It's not fair canon.
Canon Pratt	You shouldn't worry Moll. If anything happens to me you won't be forgotten. You'll get your severance pay. That will be seen to – and fifty pounds of a gift in my will to you.
Moll	Fifty pounds?
Canon Pratt	In black and white.
Moll	By God, you're a gas man with your fifty pounds – 'twould hardly buy a bicycle.
Canon Pratt	What would you say Moll, if I increased it to a hundred?
Moll	You can do the same with that as you did with the fifty – you'll have to do more.
Canon Pratt	Such as?
Moll	Such as a pension scheme and a bulk sum. Everyone gets them these days, and I'm as much entitled to them as the next person.
Canon Pratt	I've never heard the like! A bulk sum and a pension scheme? One would think you were a teacher or a higher civil servant.
Moll	If I were married to you wouldn't I have a life insurance on you? If I was your daughter wouldn't you have to give me a fortune?
Canon Pratt	We'll see, we'll see – a pension now is a different

	matter.
Moll	Them curates had a right hare made out of you before I came – you were up to your neck in debts and you were run off your feet. 'Twas me that done the worryin' and 'twas me that took charge of the bingo and the raffles. I would be expecting a pension of seven or eight pounds a week and a thousand pounds in a bulk sum.
Canon Pratt	A thousand pounds? Tell me 'tis a nightmare I'm having – where would I get a thousand pounds?
Moll	I'll show you how to make it … You can take my word for it canon, that there's a lot more in this parish than you'd think. There's them that lets on to be poor would buy and sell you. What are the people paying into Mass at present?
Canon Pratt	Two new pence.
Moll	*(Dismisses it)* That's nothing short of scandalous. Coppers for Mass, ten shillings for the dance hall. If Monsignor MacMerrigan was here he'd have 'em skinned while you'd be lookin' around you. He was a great warrant to gauge the amount of cash in a parish … and to get it out of 'em. The monsignor would never go to a pulpit. *(Imitating him)* 'I don't want to divorce myself from the people,' he used to say. 'The minute I go there Moll,' he used to say, 'I leave their world'. The monsignor knew all the tricks … He'd saunter out nice and easy, and lean back against the altar, like he'd be after meeting you in the street. Then he'd give the blessing, careless and gay and then he'd stick the two hands into the trouser pockets … *(Canon follows this*

and imitates all the actions seriously) He had a fine, soft, deep voice; very oily and greasy … 'Well, well, well, well,' he'd say, 'here we are again. What's this I'm after taking out of my trousers pocket? Ah, it's a penny! I will give this penny to this lovely girl in the front seat – but wait a minute! What an old fool I am! A penny is no use to her. If she wanted to buy sweets or an apple or an ice cream a penny would be worthless. I had better give her a shilling … So now, in the honour of God, when you come to Mass next Sunday leave the pennies at home and bring a piece of silver with you. I'll be standing at the gate myself so don't blackguard me. I'm too old for it. I don't deserve it. Forget about today. We can all make mistakes. Just get this clear; I don't want to see anyone make a mistake on Sunday next. Remember, no coppers.' *(Turns up to right)*

Canon Pratt   Did it work?

Moll   Did it what! The following Sunday the Mass contributions were trebled, and it was the same every Sunday after that. Go on canon, give it a go yourself.

(The canon steps forward and adopts the monsignor's pose. He begins confidently enough but soon degenerates into a mutter)

Canon Pratt   Well, well, well, well, here we are again. What's this I have in my trouser pocket? A penny, what have I in my other pocket? Why it's a shilling, five new pence. A penny in one hand and a shilling in the other. Um … *(He peters out)* We must go over it a few times.

Moll   Don't worry you'll have it right for Sunday. And

	another thing canon, them cards are a right money spinner.
Canon Pratt	Good Lord Moll, now you're not suggesting a poker school?
Moll	Not the playing cards – the Mass cards.
Canon Pratt	What about the Mass cards Moll?
Moll	I don't know where to start canon.
Canon Pratt	Start at the beginning Moll.
Moll	Fr Brest signed nine yesterday morning for the Mc-Goory funeral, while you were saying Mass. That's nine pounds.
Canon Pratt	Nine pounds in a morning. That's mighty money.
Moll	It should be your money canon.
Canon Pratt	He says the Masses Moll. He's entitled to the money.
Moll	Twelve times I had to answer the door for the pair of them. Most people wanting to get you to sign.
Canon Pratt	*(Thoughtfully)* That's twelve pounds between them.
Moll	And when you came back how many did you sign yourself canon?
Canon Pratt	Well now Moll, I didn't sign twelve anyway or anything near it, I may tell you.
Moll	That's what I thought canon.
Canon Pratt	*(Cutely)* And what would you recommend Moll?
Moll	'Tisn't for me to say canon.
Canon Pratt	Maybe not Moll but I may tell you I value your advice. You won't put me astray at any rate.
Moll	I'm only suggesting now, mind you.
Canon Pratt	I'm here for suggestions girl.
Moll	If you were to sign a big bundle of Mass cards and give them to me, I needn't be sending people away, saying

	you're not in or telling them to call back again. When I tell them you'll be back later they say Fr Brest will do or Fr Loran will do. That's honest money out of your pocket canon ... honest money ... You're losing hundreds canon ... hundreds ....
Canon Pratt	*(Alarmed)* Hundreds! Faith, I suppose I am.
Moll	Hundreds canon. 'Tis not unnatural for a person to be fond of money canon ... to want money in the pocket so that the house can be run and the parish can be run and all of us paid our wages. 'Tis you that pays them canon and 'tis no wonder you'd need money canon. 'Tisn't for yourself you want it.
Canon Pratt	'Tis not indeed.
Moll	'Tis no sin canon.
Canon Pratt	'Tis no sin Moll. So whoever would come to the door with money for a Mass card you would be there to meet them with the signed card.
Moll	'Tis me always answers the door canon.
Canon Pratt	'Tis a good idea God knows, but isn't there a danger Moll, that you would give my signed cards to those who would be seeking Fr Brest or Fr Loran?
Moll	I suppose it could happen all right canon. We all makes mistakes.
Canon Pratt	God help us but we do Moll. I'm sure you wouldn't do anything deliberate. You're not that sort as we all know well. *(Rubs chin)* The more I think of it the more I like it.
Moll	People set more store in a card signed by a canon than in a card signed by a curate.
Canon Pratt	I'll sign the cards first thing in the morning Moll.

Moll	*(Producing a bundle of cards)* Sure sign a few of them now canon, it will give you an appetite for your supper.
Canon Pratt	… and about our little problem …
Moll	We'll go to a solicitor and get him to draw up an agreement.
Canon Pratt	I make no promises, mind you, but allowing I could raise the thousand, I still think it's too much … We'll talk about it tomorrow.
Moll	I won't be here tomorrow morning! I'm shoving on. I'll go out in the world and find an old man that will marry me.
Canon Pratt	Moll!
Moll	An old man to marry me canon, and the older the better, because if the heart gives out on him I'll have my widow's pension, and that's a damn sight better than I'll ever see from you with your shining shoes and purple, and your grace of God.
Canon Pratt	The bishop would have to be consulted…
Moll	Will the bishop carry the breakfast up to bed to you tomorrow morning?
Canon Pratt	I'll see what can be done.
Moll	There's no seeing, you'll do it or you won't do it. If you do it I'll stay and if you don't do it I won't stay.
Canon Pratt	Be reasonable.
Moll	*(Collects duster, half goes)* I'll say goodbye to you before I go and pack my bags. All I can say is I hope you'll be lucky, and that you'll be minded half as well as I minded you. *(Sheds a tear)*
Canon Pratt	Wait! Wait a minute! Sit down, sit. It's bad to be hasty.
Moll	It is canon. You look after me, and I'll look after you.

	Look at the thousands I'll collect for you in Mass card money – sure there isn't a woman in Ireland would do as well by you.
Canon Pratt	All right, I'll do it, but you'll have to show me how. I haven't a penny, I swear it.
Moll	That's easy done. *(Stands)* Tomorrow we'll go to a solicitor and get him to draw up an agreement that whoever is parish priest after you must pay me the pension – that's important – and we'll go to the bank and raise the thousand. You'll have no bother. A parish priest's word is stronger than the Rock of Gibraltar. There's no bank manager in the world would refuse you. You put the thousand in your own name and mine with the proviso that if anything happens to you I claim it.
Canon Pratt	And if anything happens to you I can claim it.
Moll	Yes. Set yourself down there now and put your autograph on that bundle and I'll go fetch the supper. *(Moll goes to leave as the canon busies himself but on second thoughts she returns)* Er …'Tis a job you wouldn't expect me to do for nothing canon.
Canon Pratt	How's that Moll?
Moll	Giving out the cards and collecting the money for you … There's a lot of responsibility.
Canon Pratt	I'm not sure I understand you.
Moll	A commission canon?
Canon Pratt	A commission would be totally unprecedented. I declare to God but I never heard the like.
Moll	You won't lose by it canon.
Canon Pratt	What sort of commission?

Moll	A shilling in the pound, sure 'tis only five new pence. 'Tisn't much.
Canon Pratt	Moll, it's totally unprecedented.
Moll	I used to get if from Monsignor Mac Merrigan.
Canon Pratt	In that case I see no reason why you shouldn't get it from me. Five pence in the pound it will be.
Moll	I'll go and get the supper now canon.
Canon Pratt	Will you give Fr Brest a call Moll?
Moll	I will to be sure canon and would you ever ask those two buckos to tidy out their rooms? They're in an awful state altogether.
Canon Pratt	And Moll?
Moll	Yes canon.
Canon Pratt	Call him easy. He says your voice is affecting his ear-drums.
Moll	I'll call him like he was a baby canon. He's a pure baba, God help us. *(Moll laughs and is joined by the canon. Exit Moll calling out at the top of her voice. Off)* Fr Breest ... Fr Breest ... your supper is on the table ... *(Enter Fr Loran)*
Canon Pratt	And how's the choir going father?
Fr Loran	Did you ever spend two hours in a rookery canon?
Canon Pratt	Patience father, patience. We can't all be Carusos. These are simple people with no musical background. 'Tisn't a cathedral we have.
Fr Loran	Is it true you'll be getting a new organ for the church?
Canon Pratt	We'll have to ask Moll about that.
Fr Loran	Moll? Does she know something about organs?
Canon Pratt	I wouldn't say so but I'd say she knows something about the price of them.

Fr Loran	We'd badly want a new organ.
Canon Pratt	Why don't you talk to her yourself about it?
Fr Loran	I did.
Canon Pratt	And what did she say?
Fr Loran	She said I could have it if I had the price of it.
Canon Pratt	And have you the price of it?
Fr Loran	I haven't the price of a mouth organ.
Canon Pratt	I like it when a man bares his soul and says his piece.
Fr Loran	You do?
Canon Pratt	Of course.
Fr Loran	You like music don't you?
Canon Pratt	I like a good song and I like the fiddle played softly.
Fr Loran	That's not what I mean. What I mean is a massive choir drawn from the people of this parish. We don't have to confine ourselves to church music, you know.
Canon Pratt	You mean good rousing choruses like you'd hear in the pubs of a Saturday night.
Fr Loran	No. I do not. I mean one hundred men and one hundred women singing the Mass. Think of Schubert, think of Handel, think of the effect …
Canon Pratt	I don't know about Schubert, but you're off your handle all right. Do you think the people of this parish have nothing better to do?
Fr Loran	It could be done.
Canon Pratt	Choirs are all right for women that have their families reared or for young nuns that are in danger of deserting.
Fr Loran	We could give it a trial.
Canon Pratt	Sure … But wait till you have your own parish.
Fr Loran	When I have my own parish I'll have the greatest

56

choir ever heard.

Canon Pratt   By the time you have your own parish you won't have the energy.

Fr Loran   *(Places hand across stomach)* By the Lord I'm hungry. Is she looking after the supper?

Canon Pratt   We were waiting on you. She's gone calling Fr Brest.

Fr Loran   Softly, I noticed.

Canon Pratt   Now, now there's no call for sarcasm. I don't know what's gotten into the pair of you this past year.

Fr Loran   I'm not prepared to discuss it canon. I'm too weak. Discussion might only weaken me further. I'll die young. You'll find me in my bed some morning with my tongue hanging out.

(Enter Fr Brest. He seems older somehow and not as spruce as he was. His grooming is not what it was. He is bedraggled. When he enters he goes to fireplace where he elaborately extracts two gobs of cotton wool from his ears)

Fr Brest   I was upstairs resting from the fatigue of last night's bingo. Faintly, most melodiously in the distance, the gentle voices of Fr Loran's choristers sweetly assailed my ears. Ah, said I, this is sweet peace that cannot last. *(Laughs bitterly)* How right I was. Suddenly the awful shriek of Moll Kettle came to rend the silence apart. The birds were hushed. Time says I for my cotton wool.

Fr Loran   Does it soften the blow?

Fr Brest   Only a little. Nothing my dear father, is proof against the rasping screech of our dear housekeeper.

Canon Pratt	Ah! *(Enter Moll bearing plates)*
Moll	*(Loudly)* Was you asleep Fr Brest?
Fr Brest	Luckily! No.
Moll	And how is the eardrums this evening?
Fr Brest	*(Looks towards canon)* And pray who told you about my eardrums?
Moll	*(Putting down food)* Sure the whole parish knows about them. Come on the supper will be cold.
Fr Brest	And what array of delicacies are we to behold this evening?
Canon Pratt	*(Rising, rubbing his hands and taking his seat happily at table)* It's scrambled eggs on toast and it looks good. Come on lads, sit down. Fetch the tea Moll.
Moll	Here boybawn. Have a look at that while your havin' your supper.
Fr Brest	What is it?
Moll	'Tis a catalogue for the most up to date bingo ball dispensers. Turn to page fourteen and tell me what you see. *(Brest does so)* That bingo machine dispenses bingo balls of every hue. Black balls, blue balls, green balls, balls for every colour of the rainbow. *(Exits)*

(Both curates seat themselves. The canon says grace and is answered by the curates. The canon immediately plunges into supper. Fr Brest produces a pair of glasses, dons them and inspects plate with great care)

Fr Brest	What a way for an innocent egg to end up. I'm glad I'm not the hen that laid it. *(Locates slice of bread and commences to butter it. He nibbles. Enter Moll with*

	teapot. She rests it on the table. Fr Brest's eyes are glued to his plate)
Moll	*(To Brest)* Did you lose something father?
Fr Brest	Only my appetite.
Moll	Ha! You poor man, without an eardrum or an appetite. *(Exit Moll)*
Fr Brest	*(Squirming, to canon)* Did you hear that? Did you hear that canon?
Canon Pratt	Eat your supper, like a good man.
Fr Brest	You call this mess a supper.
Fr Loran	Easy Phil, easy.
Canon Pratt	*(Fed up)* What in blazes do you want? Tell us and we'll get it for you. Anything to put an end to this perpetual whining.
Fr Brest	All I want is a decent meal. I want nothing fancy.
Canon Pratt	The Lord save us, there are millions starving in India and South America …
Fr Loran	And Peru …
Canon Pratt	And Peru. Do you ever think of them?
Fr Brest	You think of them. I have enough of a problem trying to stay alive myself.
Canon Pratt	*(Clucks tongue)* Will you like a good man, will you pour out the tea Fr Loran? *(Fr Loran proceeds to pour tea)*
Fr Brest	*(Change of tactics)* Look we are three grown men and there's no reason why we should be at loggerheads. Don't you agree canon?
Canon Pratt	*(Eager to heal friction)* That's what I'm always saying. If we can't iron out our differences at our age we have failed in our calling. By God Phil, I'm with you all the

	way. Let us try to pull together rather than apart.
Fr Loran	Wisely put canon. As the hymn says – You'll never walk alone.
Canon Pratt	Yes thank you. That's the spirit. Back to the good old days again, eh. Huh? Huh?
Fr Brest	I hope so canon. I fervently hope so. But to reach any degree of happiness in any walk of life certain little sacrifices, certain acts of kindness and thoughtfulness are called for, especially if this little community of ours is to be restored to that happy state we once knew. Right?
Fr Loran	Right.
Canon Pratt	Right.
Fr Brest	What I want to know *father,* is who should make the first sacrifice? Who should set the example? *(Indicates canon)* Would you say it should come from the top or the bottom?
Fr Loran	Oh, the top … the top … where else?
Fr Brest	And who is the top? Who is the leader in this house?
Fr Loran	Moll Kettle.
Fr Brest	Don't be facetious. Our leader is our canon.
Fr Loran	Of course. *(Shouts towards kitchen)* Sorry Moll.
Fr Brest	I have already made my sacrifice. I run a regular bingo session. That, to me, is the greatest sacrifice of all.
Canon Pratt	That's not a sacrifice. That is an elementary parish duty, an evening chore.
Fr Brest	You're wrong. For me it is the great sacrifice *(Shouts)* because I hate the damned thing. I detest it. I loathe and despise it. I have frequent nightmares that are filled with numbers … red twenty-eight, green

	twenty-two, yellow fourteen, black forty-six …
Fr Loran	No. No. No, black forty-seven.
Fr Brest	Black forty-seven?
Fr Loran	Don't you get it … *(Points at plate)* the hunger … the starvation …? The great famine.
Fr Brest	Bingo will eventually be the death of me. I have become resigned to it. You have heard of the Cisco Kid, the Sundance Kid, not forgetting Billy the Kid but here before you is the original … one and only … Bingo Kid.
Canon Pratt	Might I ask what you are driving at father?
Fr Brest	Certainly canon. I am going to ask you, in the interests of harmony, to make a little sacrifice.
Canon Pratt	I'll go a reasonable length to restore harmony. What is it you expect of me?
Fr Brest	From now on canon, I want you to swap plates with me. *(There is a silence as this sinks in. Canon slowly lowers napkin with which he has been wiping his mouth. Canon's eyes fall to his own plate, slowly and move to Brest's)* It's not much. I shall endeavour to do full justice to your plate and while you are doing full justice to mine you can devote a little thought to the starving millions who are causing so much concern. *(To Loran)* What do you think father?
Fr Loran	It seems fair. It's not as if you were asking the canon to forego his meals. He will have yours.
	(Canon shattered)
Fr Brest	Exactly. Nobody can say it's unreasonable. What do you say canon? Are you prepared to make this small sacrifice?

Canon Pratt	I see nothing small about it.
Fr Brest	You don't infer then that my plate is not an adequate swap for yours?
Canon Pratt	I didn't say that.
Fr Brest	Then you agree.
Canon Pratt	Of course I agree. I've always set the lead in this presbytery.
Fr Loran	Hear. Hear. *(Hand on his shoulder)* Canon, you have taken the first important step towards a lasting peace. Would that the great powers of the world had half your courage at their peace talks.
Canon Pratt	I do what I can.
Fr Loran	*(Carried away)* Let's shake hands on it.
	(All shake)
Canon Pratt	*(Standing, rubs hands)* Ah, this is great. I am very happy lads, very happy indeed. And now I'm going to ask the two of you to make a little sacrifice ....
Fr Loran	Anything canon, anything.
Canon Pratt	As you both know Moll is not getting younger. What she really needs is a little serving girl to do the beds and shine the windows.
Fr Brest	Yes of course.
Canon Pratt	She refuses, however, to allow a girl inside the door. The poor woman is genuinely overworked and God knows 'tis hardly fair to her if you know what I mean ...
Fr Brest	What do you mean canon?
Canon Pratt	Suppose the two of you were to make your own beds and be responsible for the tidiness of your own rooms. She says that this would be a great help to her.

Fr Brest	Canon I am a priest not a parlour maid … I … I …
Fr Loran	Take it easy Phil. It's not so awful. Any fool can make a bed. It's reasonable enough.
Canon Pratt	Well Philip?
Fr Brest	All right. I won't spoil sport.
Canon Pratt	*(Sits)* There are good times coming. Thanks be to the good God, say I. *(Enter Moll)*
Moll	There's some apple pie and custard if anyone would care for some.
Fr Brest	Bring it on woman. Bring it on. *(Rubbing hands and going to table. Exit Moll. Sitting down, spoon in one hand, fork in the other)* Even as a child I had a particular longing for apple pie and custard. My mother used to specialise in apple pies. I must get her to send you one canon.
Canon Pratt	That would be nice.
Fr Brest	*(Extremely good cheer)* We had our own orchard, still have in fact. It's a wonder you never thought of planting a few fruit trees canon.
Canon Pratt	No time.
Fr Brest	There's a good market for fresh fruit. *(Enter Moll, bearing a tray on which there are three dessert plates. She places one in front of each, the canon first, Fr Loran second, and Fr Brest third)*
Moll	*(To canon)* One for the master. *(Places plate in front of him)* One for the dame. *(She places plate in front of him)* And one for the little boy that lives down the lane. *(She places largest plate in front of Fr Brest)*
Fr Brest	*(Rubs his hands)* This is fabulous. This is the loveliest and the largest dish of apple pie and custard I have

	ever seen. Thank you Moll.
Moll	Don't mention it father.
Fr Brest	*(Seizing spoon and adjusting himself on chair)* This is really something. *(The canon coughs politely in Fr Brest's direction)* Yes canon?

(The canon points at Fr Brest's plate and then points at himself with a most polite smile. Fr Brest is puzzled. Canon hands his plate to Fr Brest. Brest accepts it, still wondering. Then it dawns on him. He lifts his own plate and reluctantly hands it to the canon who accepts it cheerily. Canon wires into it watched by Brest and Loran. Moll laughs and exits)

BRIDGE ACT TWO, SCENE ONE TO SCENE TWO

Canon Pratt   They happen all around us every day but mostly we don't even recognise them. I am talking about God's little miracles. *(Enter Bridgie, heavily pregnant)* There's a saying to cover it, what in blazes is it now…? Oh, yes, 'God works in mysterious ways'. You've often heard that said, no doubt. Well, 'tis none the less true for that.

Sure who'd have thought that Fr Loran, a man without the echo of a note in his head, would be after running a choir? God alone knows. And He must have given the hint to Moll Kettle for wasn't it she who organised it?

Oh, yes, there was a great deal of honest activity going on in Ballast during Moll's time at the presbytery. And thanks be to God, says I.

Moll reads the paper by the fire. Fr Brest tries fixing his bingo machine.

Moll   *(Referring to the paper)* There's a picture in here of the new school. Wasn't it a lucky day the canon hired me four years ago! Look what I done. I built as fine a school as you'd see in Ireland and today 'tis being opened. 'Tis a great pity the bishop can't be here … but sure we can't have everything.

Fr Brest   You really think it was you and you alone who built the school?

65

Moll	'Twas me and the bingo.
Fr Brest	Bingo … the ultimate role of the Catholic Church in Ireland … the propagation of bingo.
Moll	May God forgive you.
Fr Brest	Where's the canon?
Moll	Bed.
Fr Brest	This hour of the day? Is he sick or what?
Moll	He's fine boybawn, thanks be to God. He's resting for the celebrations. I don't see your name here.
Fr Brest	Where?
Moll	The new list of diocesan appointments.
Fr Brest	How in the name of God would my name be there when old fogies of eighty and more won't give up the ghost? You'd think they would have the grace to retire and give the younger men a chance.
Moll	A chance at what?
Fr Brest	A chance to prove ourselves, to bring decaying parishes up-to-date, to get with it.
Moll	A lot you did with this decaying parish until I arrived and a lot you'd do now if you were let at it yourself. Where would you get the money?
Fr Brest	*(Bluffing)* God is good.
Moll	And bingo is good and raffles is good and jumble sales is good.
Fr Brest	*(Getting up)* Yirra, jumble rubbish … By the way, did you see my golf clubs anywhere?
Moll	Golf clubs? Yirra you have no time for golf boybawn, the man that has 'em now has his handicap down to nine.
Fr Brest	Haw?

Moll	And they raised three ten for the new school.
Fr Brest	Do you mean to stand there and tell me …?
Moll	Yirra blast you, what do I care about you?
Fr Brest	That's a nice way to address a priest.
Moll	If you don't learn how to master that contraption your balls will be all over the place tonight.
Fr Brest	Oh dear God but you're a terrible creature altogether but the Church will master you in the end.
Moll	And pray what have I to do with the Church? Sure an altar boy is higher up in the Church than I am.
Fr Brest	There's one great consolation.
Moll	What would that be?
Fr Brest	When the canon's day comes you're for the high jump. You'll go the road of Hitler and Stalin and all the other tyrants.
Moll	If I do I'll have something to show for my time.
Fr Brest	You don't have to tell me. By God you must have a right few quid made out of the Mass cards *(Looking back at her),* not to mention the butcher and the baker and the grocer and any place else you could rob a halfpenny.
Moll	I have as much rights as you have and when you're going to the bishop let me know and I'll go with you. And if you're not satisfied with the bishop we'll go to the cardinal and if you're not satisfied with the cardinal we'll go to the pope.
Fr Brest	You're mad, stone mad.
Moll	Come on. You're the one that wanted to go to the bishop, aren't you? Always talking about it behind my back. Come on and we'll tell him that there's a new

school since I came to this parish and we'll tell him the church is repaired and all the debts paid, all since I came.

Fr Brest It was our work, mine and Fr Loran's.

(Enter Fr Loran, coatless and wearing dust turban. He carries a vacuum cleaner under his arm and a mop and pail in his hand)

Fr Loran I've just done my room. Do you want me to do yours?

Fr Brest No thank you.

Fr Loran I'll give it a hoover so.

Fr Brest I'm all right. I told you I can pull my weight.

Fr Loran You mustn't fret yourself.

Fr Brest I'm not fretting myself. *(Indicates Moll)* This monster here has me upset. She won't rest happy till she has me under the clay.

Fr Loran Now, now, Phil, you mustn't let her get at you. I just ignore her.

Moll Listen to the Mohammedan with the turban on his poll. A pity the bishop couldn't see you now.

Fr Loran *(Mustering dignity)* Varium et mutabile semper femina.

Fr Brest Well spoken Fr Loran.

Moll *(In spite)* In nomina domina gomina, goose-grease galorum, sago lumbago tapioca semolina and if you don't like the music you can change the band, and if you're going to do any hoovering here boybawn forget it. I want to have a snooze before the festivities.

(Fr Loran hoovers; Fr Brest busies himself about his bingo machine and Moll after a few moments looking at the

paper appears to doze off. As the hoovering stops Brest and Loran are struck by the silence in the room and eventually focusing on Moll they realise she is asleep, the newspaper covering her face)

Fr Brest Look at her. You'd swear butter wouldn't melt in her mouth. The devil incarnate.

Fr Loran The devil?

Fr Brest Who but a devil or an evil spirit would interfere with my sermon on mixed marriages? 'Mixed marriages how are you?' says she, ''twould be more in your line to give a sermon on mixed bread'.

Fr Loran *(Now moving in closer to Moll)* Phil, maybe she is possessed.

Fr Brest The devil has more sense.

Fr Loran No seriously, she's dozing. This may be the only chance we ever have to exorcise her.

(Fr Brest is about to protest but Loran is gone like a shot to get the accoutrements for the exorcism. Brest remains sceptical but interested throughout the following. Loran re-enters wearing purple stole and carrying a lit candle and holy water font and sprinkler. Still wearing the apron and turban from his cleaning duties, he cuts a bizarre figure)

Fr Brest I don't like this one bit. Maybe it might be better if we made contact with the official diocesan exorcist.

Fr Loran He'd never agree and she'd never submit. We'd have to tie her down.

Fr Brest Suppose something goes wrong!

Fr Loran It's a chance we have to take. Look it's for her own good. There's no doubt but she's possessed. There's no other explanation for her diabolical behaviour. Here … hold this. *(He hands him holy water vat and sprinkler. Fr Loran finds book in his vestments and, wetting his thumb, locates appropriate page. He approaches Moll and removes the newspaper. She stirs uneasily but does not wake. Solemnly Fr Loran dips his sprinkler into the holy water vat. Moll opens her eyes while their backs are turned, looks up and falls quickly back to pretended sleep again)*

Fr Brest The room first. *(Fr Loran dutifully sprinkles the entire room before addressing himself to Moll. He mutters some Latin while sprinkling. He gently sprinkles Moll. She stirs but does not waken)* Easy for God's sake.

Fr Loran O Lord we call on you now in our hour of great need, to rescue us from Satan and his minions. We ask you to free your poor servant Moll Kettle from the devil's tricks, that she might return to the path of goodness, gentleness, meekness. *(Moll opens her eyes and staring demoniacally at Brest and Loran chases them from the room. Collapses laughing in the chair as the canon enters)*

Canon Pratt I brought you these empties, save you the trouble of getting them yourself.

Moll There was no need to do that. Sit down by the fire and read your paper.

Canon Pratt Anything good in it?

Moll The pope says the world has gone to the dogs.

Canon Pratt My mother used to say the same thing when I was a child.

Moll People has no conscience these days.

Canon Pratt Too well I know it.

Moll	Where's it going to end canon, with the women going around half naked? *(Canon clucks tongue reproachfully and nods his head in agreement)* They'll be wearing nothing at all soon.
Canon Pratt	The country is too cold for that.
Moll	When I was a girl, walking the streets with my friends, you would hear the hum of the holy Rosary from every home.
Canon Pratt	My God, yes.
Moll	And the beads rattling like horses' tackling. 'Tis the Beatles you'd hear now. *(The canon settles himself in his chair and reads his newspaper. There's a momentary lull)*
Canon Pratt	Where were Frs Brest and Loran rushing off to Moll?
Moll	*(Twinkle in her eye)* The divil only knows canon.
Canon Pratt	They're very agitated these days Moll.
Moll	The Lord save us all canon, there's no meaning in the curates that's going these days. There's none of 'em want to do what they're told. Fr Brest is as bold as brass. God be with the fine curates we had when I was young. Pure saints they were with the eyes gone back in their heads and black rings under them like they'd be painted. Skin and bone and thin white faces, with the cheekbones standing out like corpses. 'Tis they were the holy men and 'twasn't their bellies was troubling them.
Canon Pratt	'Twas not indeed.
Moll	I remember one of Monsignor Mac Merrigan's first curates. You would swear he was after being whitewashed, the creature was so pale. He couldn't

talk, only whisper. The Lord save us, but I tried every shop in the diocese to find a collar small enough for his neck. Sure he had no neck canon. 'Twas all Adam's apple. I often saw him stagger with the weakness on a cold morning …

Canon Pratt Where's he now Moll?

Moll He's in heaven canon. Where the hell else would he be!

Canon Pratt Where else indeed, the poor man.

Moll A canon now is different.

Canon Pratt What should he be like now Moll? *(Preens himself)*

Moll He should be fat and pleasant with a fine red face and a deep voice, like a bull, to frighten the sinners and to give the people confidence. Sure you would never see a thin canon. What would the people think if he wasn't round and shining and in prime condition.

Canon Pratt Go on, go on.

Moll A canon now should be a fine, rumbling, thundering man, well-fed and groomed so that his parish could boast of his appearance and be proud of him. He should have a fine thick neck, a severe face and a noble bearing to give him weight and holiness. Yourself now canon, is a fine example of what a canon should look like. Show me the priest, the monsignor used to say, and I'll tell you what the parish is like.

Canon Pratt *(Preens himself)* I dare say there's a lot in what you say Moll. God knows you're not a woman that's given to exaggeration. I suppose there's no one would say that I'm not cut out for my job.

Moll There's no one would deny it canon, no one. God

	save us but them curates of ours is a pure disgrace, that would eat you out of house and home instead of fasting and abstaining like the saints and martyrs.
Canon Pratt	Now, now, Moll, we mustn't be hard.
Moll	When I was handing up Brest his dinner the day you were away, he says to me, 'Where's the soup?' 'What soup is that boybawn?' I said to him. 'The soup before lunch,' says he. 'Soup is for invalids,' I told him. 'That's me,' says he. I tell you canon, when they start looking for soup before their dinner, they'll be looking for it after their dinner, sure isn't soup a dinner in itself canon?
Canon Pratt	A good plate of soup can be most nourishing.
	(Enter Fr Brest in an excited state)
Fr Brest	The bishop! The bishop!
Canon Pratt	What about the bishop?
Fr Brest	The bishop, he's coming.
Canon Pratt	Sure he can't be coming, sure isn't he way out foreign someplace.
Fr Brest	Well he's here now.
Canon Pratt	Oh Moll, there's nothing ready.
Moll	Calm down canon, calm down.
Fr Loran	His lordship, the bishop.

(Enter a bishop in full regalia and humour. He is the master of the diocese)

Bishop	*(To Moll and canon)* Don't stand up. Don't stand up. You're looking well Connie. *(Expansively. As the canon kisses his ring)* None of that. No need for that.

Canon Pratt	A drink Moll. Get a drink for his lordship. A drink for everybody. Paddy Flaherty isn't it my lord?
Bishop	Yes. A drop of Paddy. Take a little wine Saint Paul says, for thy stomach's sake and for thy frequent infirmities. *(Exit Moll)* I was in Morocco. I woke up yesterday evening after lunch and looked out over the Mediterranean. This is very nice, very nice, I told myself, but isn't something happening in another part of the world? Isn't a school about to be opened, I said to myself. Isn't it about to be opened in my own diocese and isn't it to be opened by a substitute? Time I said to myself to be hitting for the green isle of Erin. Here I am ….

(All applaud)

Fr Loran	Marvellous! Marvellous!
Fr Brest	To cut short his holiday.
Canon Pratt	It's what we expect of the man.
Fr Loran	Imagine from Morocco to Ballast!
Bishop	*(To canon)* It's a great credit to you Canon Pratt. Four years ago we had a ramshackle outhouse where you would be ashamed to send a decent scholar. *(To window. Looks out)* Now we have a school second to none. I am not unmindful of builders, those who further the cause of education are always in my mind, if you know what I mean. *(Enter Moll, bearing a tray on which are glasses. Puts tray and glasses on right of table near bishop. Whiskey on tray. Brest pours out drinks, gives one to bishop. Moll takes glass off table and gives it to canon)*

74

Moll	*(Distributing drinks)* Now would anyone like a drop of soup to keep them going till the festivities begin?
Bishop	Pray who have we here?
Canon Pratt	This is our housekeeper my lord.

(Brest brings Loran down to left and is obviously arguing with him. 'Now is the time', Loran demurs)

Bishop	So this is Moll. *(Puts out hand, Moll kisses ring)*
Canon Pratt	You know of her?
Bishop	*(Retaining Moll's hand)* We know more than we are supposed to know Canon Pratt. *(Slaps her hand)* I have heard great accounts of Moll. *(Pats her shoulder, ushering her off)* Moll, fetch a drink for yourself and then we will all toast the great centre of education which is about to be declared open.
Moll	Yes, my Lord. *(Exit Moll)*
Bishop	*(To curates)* And now gentlemen, what's the score with the pair of you?

(Suddenly faces them. Brest rather quickly and suddenly turns)

Fr Brest	We're fine, fine, my Lord.
Bishop	No grievances?
Fr Loran	No ... no ... not at all.
Bishop	A presbytery without grievances is paradise. Paradise does not come until we visit the next world. Speak up gentlemen.
Fr Loran	*(Prompted by Fr Brest)* Well, there's never a rose without a thorn your lordship.

Canon Pratt	*(Interjects)* They're always hopping balls my lord! Look at them. Did you ever see such health?
Fr Brest	Go on Joe. *(Loran hesitates. Brest fumes and is about to explode)* As the senior curate in this parish I …
Moll	*(Entering)* Here I am canon.
Canon Pratt	Will you be toastmaster my lord? Joe, will you like a good man get the parish camera, we'll record this for posterity. You don't mind my lord?
Bishop	Certainly not. Moll! *(Bishop beckons Moll over for photo)*
Moll	Me!
Bishop	Ladies and gentlemen, I bid you toast our new school. Long may it stand and may the scholars pour forth from its portals until Gabriel sounds his horn. Go maire sé go deo is go dtiocfaidh na scoláirí ó na hallaí ina sluaite. *(All quaff. Exit Moll)*
Fr Brest	My lord you asked earlier if we had any grievances. Well on our behalf Fr Loran would like to say a few words about conditions in this presbytery. Fr Loran?

(Again Loran hesitates)

Bishop	*(To Loran)* Well what have you to say?
Fr Loran	What do you want me to say my lord?
Bishop	Say what's in your mind. Be frank. Be candid.
Fr Loran	Be candid about what my lord?
Bishop	About conditions in this presbytery.
Fr Loran	*(Unctuous)* I have no complaints my lord. I am only a curate.
Fr Brest	Only a curate … Tell him the truth ….

Fr Loran	*(All innocence)* The truth is my lord, that I personally have no complaints to make.
Fr Brest	Judas. Judas Iscariot.
Bishop	In a few moments I will be opening a new school, and after that I must go to suppress a Women's Lib movement in Lyracrompane. But I cannot leave unless there is peace in this house.
	In Morocco I had time to think. *(To canon, turns to canon)* Canon Pratt you have served this diocese well. You have lived in obscurity in this out-of-the-way place for far too long. You have brought this parish out of the doldrums. You have given it a new school, a new status. You are the kind of canon who deserves better. *(Moves to canon, hand on shoulder)* For this reason I am appointing you to the parish of St Andrew in the city. You'll be happy there. I am sure that in no time at all you will be made a monsignor. It will be nice to have you near me in the city. *(Moves casually back to table)* Your age and experience will be assets to the diocese. *(Enter Moll. Bearing canon's comb, collar, surplice, and hat)*
Canon Pratt	I don't know what to say ... a monsignor ... St Andrew's ... Am I hearing things? Moll, do you hear this? We are bound for the city ....
Bishop	*(Turns: definitely)* You didn't hear me right father. You are bound for the city. Moll is not bound anywhere.
Canon Pratt	But ...
Bishop	*(Hand raised)* Let there be no buts. The parish of Saint Andrew is run by an order of nuns.
Canon Pratt	But we've been together for so long.

Bishop	*(Facing canon)* The Church is a hard master canon, but hard as it is it isn't half as hard as a community of nuns. I would face the fires of hell on top of a bucking bronco before I would face a rampaging reverend mother. Moll stays here. Her assistance will be vital. The new parish priest will have a tough task before him.
Canon Pratt	Have you somebody in mind?
Bishop	Indeed I have. *(Turns: he looks at Fr Brest)* You may say I have. *(Fr Brest opens his mouth in astonishment and foolishly points a finger towards himself)*
Fr Brest	*(Disbelief)* Me?
Bishop	Who else father? *(Fr Brest staggers with the shock of it. He is supported by Fr Loran)*
Bishop	Fr Loran you will now be the senior curate. I will appoint a junior curate in due course.
Fr Loran	Is there any hope of a transfer my lord? *(Bishop laughs)* Oh God! If I knew the day I was ordained what was before me I'd have jacked the whole thing up and become a christian brother. Anything is better than being a curate.
Fr Brest	There are worse things in life father.
Fr Loran	*(Faces Fr Brest)* Name them.
Fr Brest	We'll have good times now Joe. Not to worry.
Bishop	Well canon. Shall we be on our way? There's a school to be opened and I'd like to see it first.

(Fr Loran opens door. They pass down stage of Fr Brest who moves up, if necessary, to make room for them. Bishop goes to door. Canon follows fairly slowly. Fr Brest a little to right, where canon blesses him)

Canon Pratt	Of course my Lord. *(They are about to exit)* Oh, and, Moll – see the new parish priest about that 'little arrangement'. *(Exit canon)*
Fr Brest	What 'little arrangement'?
Moll	I'll talk to you later father.
Bishop	I'm sure you will. Has anyone any more to say? Come on. Now's the time. 'Tis no good talking about a bishop behind his back. All right then. May God's blessing be always on your ministry here Fr Brest. Be patient with your curates, thankful to your housekeeper and remember that incredible though it may seem now, I was once a curate too. God bless ye. *(Exit bishop)*
Fr Loran	You came out of it nicely.
Fr Brest	I was the senior curate.
Fr Loran	And I the junior.
Fr Brest	So long as you remember that we'll get on fine.
Fr Loran	I never thought I'd see the day.
Moll	'Twill be the best part of an hour before the school is opened. Will you take a drop of soup? I have it ready.
Fr Brest	All right all right. Let's have some soup. *(Exit Moll)* This will be a model parish. The new community centre will be an example to the rest of the country.
Fr Loran	Where will you get the money?
Fr Brest	I'll get it from the greatest source of all – from bingo. From now on we'll have bingo every night but it will be a bigger and a better bingo. *(Enter Moll with tray and two bowls of soup. One small, one large)* You hear me Moll, a bigger and better bingo.
Moll	I declare to God but you'll make a great parish priest entirely.

Fr Loran	How come we have different amounts?
Moll	What are you talking about?
Fr Loran	He has twice as much soup as I have.
Moll	If you don't like it, leave it.
Fr Loran	You saw the amount I got.
Fr Brest	In the name of God man I can't be bothered with these trifles. I have a big parish to run. You want to watch yourself, fall into line fast. I have only so much patience. Up to your organ loft and get the hang of this yoke between hymns. Bingo is now part of your job. Off you go now. *(Hands him the bingo machine)*
Fr Loran	A curate's lot is a hard one … *(Opens door)* there's no doubt but the curates of this country should be canonised. Canonised. *(Exits as bingo balls erupt from the machine)*
Fr Brest	It's not going to be easy Moll. That new community centre will cost money.
Moll	Put your legs up there and rest yourself. We have our bingo and what's to stop us having silver circles and raffles? If the money is there we'll get it out of them. You look out for me father and I'll look out for you and let the curates of this world look after themselves.

CURTAIN